nickelodeon™

DORA the EXPLORER™

Princess Dreams

A GOLDEN BOOK • NEW YORK

ISBN: 978-0-375-85952-6

www.randomhouse.com/kids

ROYAL DANCE

¡Hola! I'm Dora and this is Boots. One time, we used our dancing to save Swiper the Fox. Here's the story.

Swiper finds a magic bottle with a little Dancing Elf trapped inside. The elf doesn't have enough room to dance inside the bottle and wants to get out.

The Dancing Elf tricks Swiper into switching places with him. So now we need one big wish to get Swiper out of the magic bottle. We can get one big wish at the Castle. *¡Vámonos!* Let's go!

To get to the Castle, we have to go through the Pyramid and then cross the Ocean.

Hooray for Tico!
He can get us to the Pyramid fast in his airplane.

We made it to the Pyramid! To get through it,
we have to march like ants. Will you march like an ant?

Next, we have to wiggle our arms like spiders.
Will you wiggle, too? Now we have to slither and
slide like a sneaky snake. Slither and slide!
Great dancing!

We danced through the Pyramid! Now Isa will get us
to the Ocean fast on her bicycle.
We're on our way to wish Swiper free!
Pedal, pedal, pedal!

Look! It's the Pirate Piggies!
They can help us get across the Ocean.

Oh, no! Swiper fell into that whale's mouth!
We need to sprinkle some pepper onto the whale.
Then he'll sneeze out Swiper.

We made it to the Castle and we're just in time for the Royal Dance Contest! The winner gets one big wish! But first we need some fancy clothes.

Benny is bringing us some fancy clothes!

Wow! We look great!
Now we can dance in the contest and win one big wish for Swiper!

The silly King is starting the contest.
Let's dance!

We won the Royal Dance Contest and the wish!
Now we can wish Swiper free!

The Dancing Elf tells Swiper he's sorry. Swiper doesn't have to go back into the bottle. We all dance to celebrate. We couldn't have done it without you!

PRINCESS FOR A DAY

¡Hola! Boots and I are dancing in the ballet today.
I get to play the part of the princess!

Boots is so graceful!

Draw a line connecting the dance moves on the left to the matching shapes on the right.

Follow the path marked DANCE to help Dora get to school.

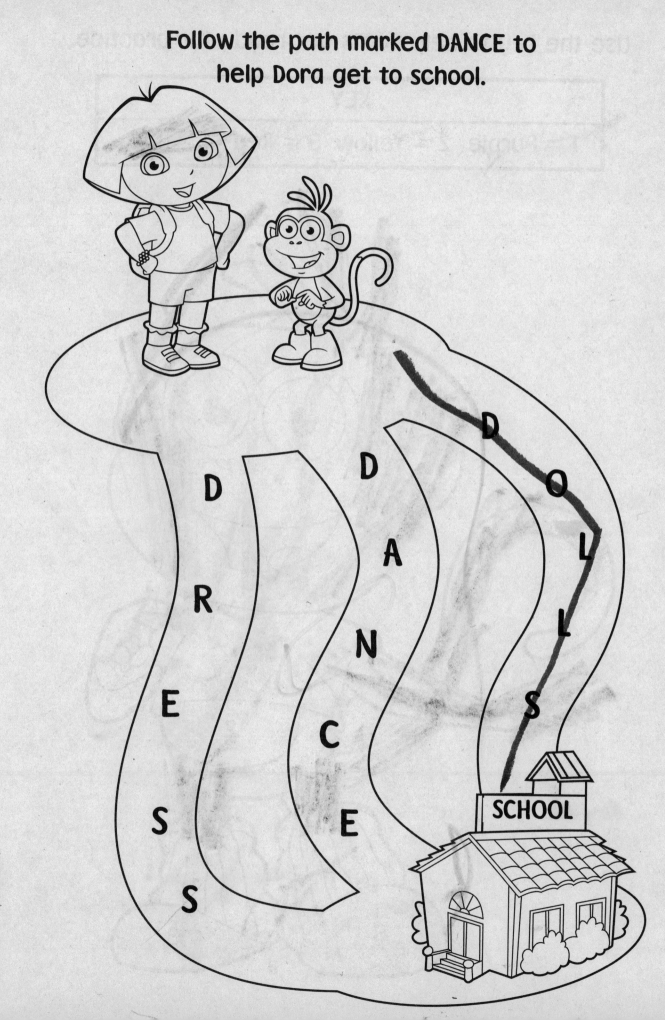

Use the key to help Boots get ready for practice.

Look at this page. Then look at the next one.
How many differences can you find?

ANSWER: On this page, the gym bag is now in the room; Swiper is missing; there is another shoe; and there is a soccer ball.

A princess needs a tiara. Will you draw one on Dora?

Come on! Let's dance! *¡Vamos a bailar!*

Wow, Boots and Isa are wonderful dance partners!

Mami and Papi are so proud of me!

Take a bow, everyone!

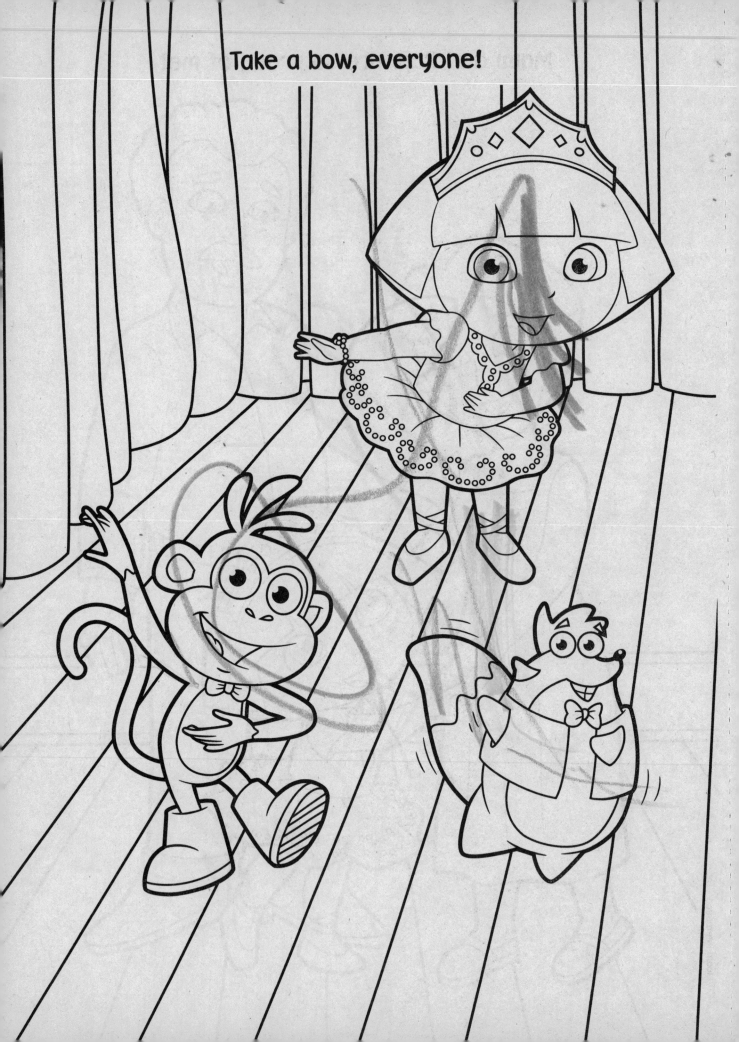

Use the key to color these flowers for Dora.

KEY
1 = Green 2 = Yellow 3 = Red 4 = Blue

Thank you for all your help.
I really loved dancing with you.

THE MERMAID PRINCESS

¡Hola, soy Dora! And this is Boots! Today is Clean Up the Beach Day. Will you help us make the beach clean?

Help us by circling the things that do not belong on the beach.

¡Mira! It's a special clam. If we use the magic word to get him to open, he'll tell us his story.

We've got to say the Spanish word for "open."
Say "¡Abre!"

Look! The clam is opening!

Deep inside the ocean was the Mermaid Kingdom,
where everyone was happy as can be.

But then a mean old Octopus dumped garbage over the Mermaid Kingdom!

A young mermaid named Mariana found
a magic crown. She made a wish, and all
the garbage was gone.

One day, a wave washed the Mermaid Crown away!

Now garbage is piling up in the Mermaid Kingdom!

That's a sad story! Mariana needs her
Mermaid Crown to make the garbage go away.
Do you see the Mermaid Crown?

We found the crown! *¡La corona!*
Will you help us bring it back to Mariana?

Map says we have to go over Seashell Bridge, across Pirate Island, and past the Silly Sea to get to the Mermaid Kingdom.

We need to find Seashell Bridge.
Do you see the path that leads to it?

To cross the bridge, we have to follow the shells from 1 to 6. Wait, do you hear something?

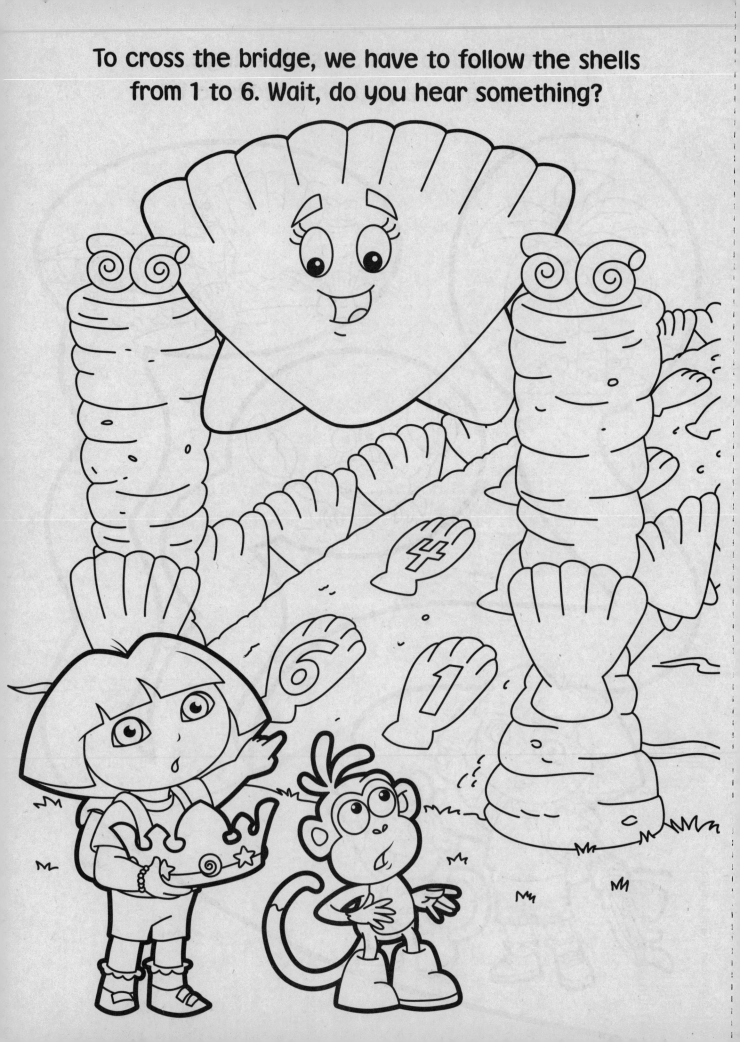

Uh-oh! That sounds like the Octopus.

He's putting dirt on the shells! If we can't see the
numbers, we can't find our way
to the Mermaid Kingdom!

We need to clean the dirt off the shells! Will you check Backpack and circle something we can use?

Help Boots vacuum up the dirt.
Say "Vroom, vroom, vroom!"

The bridge is clean!
Count with me! *¡Uno, dos, tres, cuatro, cinco, seis!*

We made it over Seashell Bridge! Next we go
to Pirate Island. Do you see Pirate Island?

Hey, I think that rock is following us!

Oh, no! That's not a rock—that's Swiper!
He's swiping the Mermaid Crown!

Swiper, wait! That's Mariana's Mermaid Crown.
She needs it to wish the Mermaid Kingdom clean!

Swiper is giving back the crown! Swiper really likes
swiping, but he really, really likes the mermaids.

We made it to Pirate Island!
Uh-oh, the Coconut Trees won't let us by.

The Pirate Pig says the Coconut Trees
will let us by if we dance the Coconut Conga.

Will you dance the Coconut Conga with us?
Say *"¡Conga!"* to get the trees to move.

The Silly Sea is next! But there's mean old Octopus,
and he's heading for the Mermaid Kingdom.
We've got to hurry!

There are some dolphins who swim in these waters. Let's call my cousin Diego. He can ask the dolphins to give us a ride across! Say "Diego!"

¡Hola, Dora! Hi, Boots!

Let's call to the dolphins. Say "Squeak, squeak!"

Here they come!

¡*Gracias*, Diego! Come on, we've got to bring the magic Mermaid Crown back to Mariana.

¡Hola, Mariana! I'm Dora, and this is Boots.
We found your magic Mermaid Crown.

Oh, no! The mean Octopus!

The Octopus has trapped Mariana in his net!

We've got to catch the Mermaid Crown
so we can wish the Mermaid Kingdom clean.

Oooh! The magic Mermaid Crown turned me into a mermaid! I wish to get rid of the garbage and save the Mermaid Kingdom!

Look, some of the garbage is disappearing,
but there's so much, the magic isn't enough!

We need help from all our friends!
Clean up, clean up, everybody clean up!

We did it! The Mermaid Kingdom is clean!

The Octopus is really, really sorry. From now on,
he'll put all the garbage in the garbage dump.
And he's going to recycle!

Mariana, I love being a mermaid, but I have to go home. This is your crown. You need it to protect the Mermaid Kingdom.

Mariana has a mermaid necklace for me.
I can put it on and visit her anytime!

We couldn't have done it without you.
Thanks for helping! *¡Gracias!*

THE SNOW PRINCESS

¡Hola, soy Dora!
I'm going to read from my storybook.
Do you like books?

We love books!
¡Nos encantan los libros!

My friends want to hear a story about a snow
princess and a fairy snowflake . . .

. . . with pirates and a mean witch, too.
Let's see if I have a story like that.

Do you see pictures of a snow princess and a witch? Circle them.

Once upon time, there was a little girl named Sabrina who loved snow. She lived in a lonely, dry forest, where it never snowed.

One day, Sabrina found a white dove that had been caught in a witch's trap. No one would set the dove free because they were afraid of the witch.

But Sabrina set the dove free, and the dove
rewarded her with a magic crystal.

When Sabrina looked into the crystal and smiled,
something amazing happened—it snowed!

And the dove turned into a Snow Fairy. The Snow Fairy gave Sabrina a beautiful snow-crystal gown and made her the Snow Princess. Does the princess look like anyone you know?

The Snow Princess made friends with all the animals in the Snowy Forest.

But there was a mean Witch who didn't like the
Snowy Forest. And she didn't like how happy
the Princess and her friends were.

The Witch took the magic crystal, then waved her
wand and hid the Snow Princess on the
roof of a faraway tower.

The Witch looked into the crystal and made
a mean face. She flew away as the
Snowy Forest started to melt.

Everyone looked for the Snow Princess, but they couldn't find her. They needed her to bring back the snow!

Look! The Snow Fairy is jumping out of the book.
He thinks I'm the Snow Princess!

The Snow Fairy needs to find the Snow Princess, or the Snowy Forest will melt away and disappear forever. We have to help him!

We all have to jump into the book!

We made it into the Snowy Forest.
How will we find the Snow Princess?

Who do we ask for help when we don't know which way to go?

Map, right! Map says we have to go across the Icy
Ocean, past the Snow Hills, and through the Cave.
That's how we'll get to the Princess!

We made it to the Icy Ocean. Look! Some of the ice
is melting. We'd better hurry and rescue the Princess.
We need to find a boat!

A boat! ¡Un barco!

It's the Pirate Piggies! We've got to call them!
Say "Pirate Piggies!"

The Pirate Piggies can sail us across the Icy Ocean!
Let's go save *la Princesa.*

Will you connect the dots to raise the sail?

**Oh, no! Here comes the Witch.
She's going to try to stop us from saving the Princess!**

The Witch has sent an Icy Sea Snake to stop us!

All sea snakes are afraid of pirates!
To scare away the snake, make a pirate
face and say *"Arrr!"*

Woo-hoo! We really scared him!
Now let's go save *la Princesa*.

It shouldn't be much longer before we reach the Snow Hills. I hope we don't crash into any—ICEBERGS!

Oh, no! Boots was knocked overboard, and his boots are stuck to that ice! He's floating away.

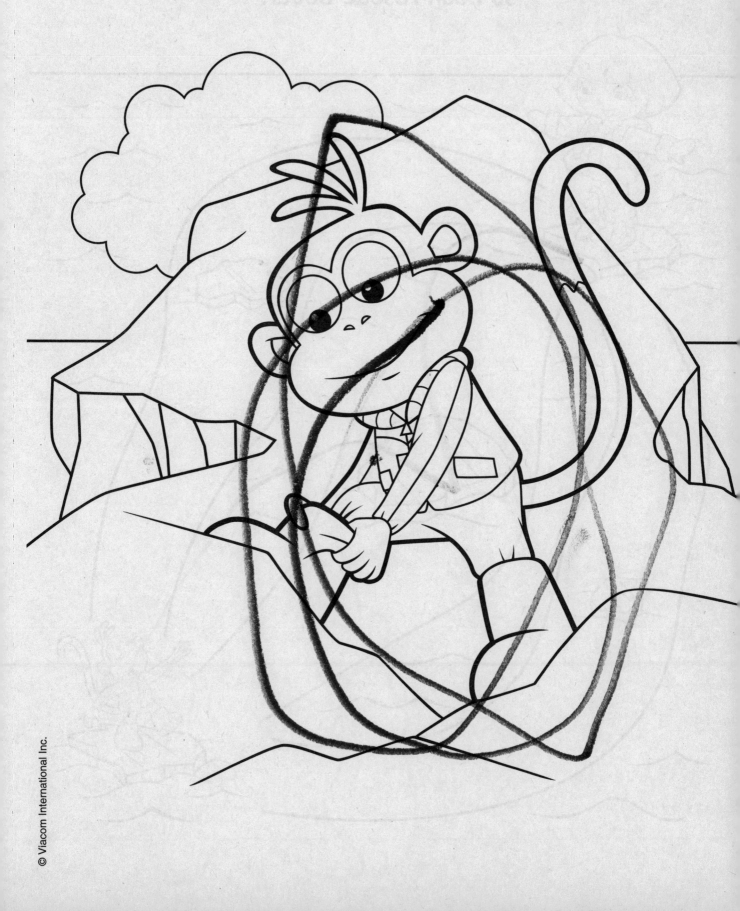

The ice I'm on is melting. I need to find a bigger piece. Will you find the biggest piece of ice so I can rescue Boots?

You're safe now, Boots!
And we made it across the Icy Ocean!

Next we need to go to the Snow Hills.
Do you see them?

You found the Snow Hills.
Come on! *¡Vámonos!*

That lly monkey thinks he's the king of that snow hill!

The Witch turned the snow hill into an angry polar bear!

Look! It's an Inuit girl driving a dogsled.
Maybe she can help us.

Paj is giving us a ride on her sled.
Say *"Chuk, chuk!"* to make her dogs run faster
so we can get away from the polar bear.

Will you help us find the path that leads through the Snow Hills? Watch out for the polar bear.

Wow, Paj really knows how to get away from polar bears. And we made it past the Snow Hills!

Next we go to the Cave.
Paj will get us there superfast!

We made it to the Cave.
Thanks for all your help, Paj.

Oh, no! The wind blew the Snow Fairy into the Cave!

We've got to find the Snow Fairy.
Let us know if you see him.

The Snow Fairy looks smaller. I think he's melting.
We'd better rescue the Princess so she can
make it snow. Then the Snow Fairy will grow
bigger and stronger.

We've got to get out of this Cave.
Do you see a way out?

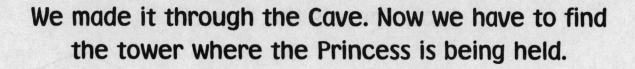

We made it through the Cave. Now we have to find
the tower where the Princess is being held.

Look! There's the tower!

We need to get down the Snowy Mountain fast!
Will you check Backpack for something we can use
to get down the mountain?

I'm Backpack. Will you circle something Dora and Boots can use to slide down the Snowy Mountain?

Smart thinking. On this snowboard, we can slide right down! Wheee!

Watch out! The snow has melted up ahead.
To help us jump over the rocks, say "Jump!"

Will you help us find the path to the tower at the bottom of the mountain? Watch out for rocks!

We made it over the rocks!
And look, there's the Princess!

The drawbridge is up! How will we get to the Princess?

The Snow Fairy can fly over and pull the switch that brings the drawbridge down!

The Snow Fairy has melted so much that he can barely fly. To fix his wings, connect the numbered dots from 1 to 10, then the lettered dots from A to J.

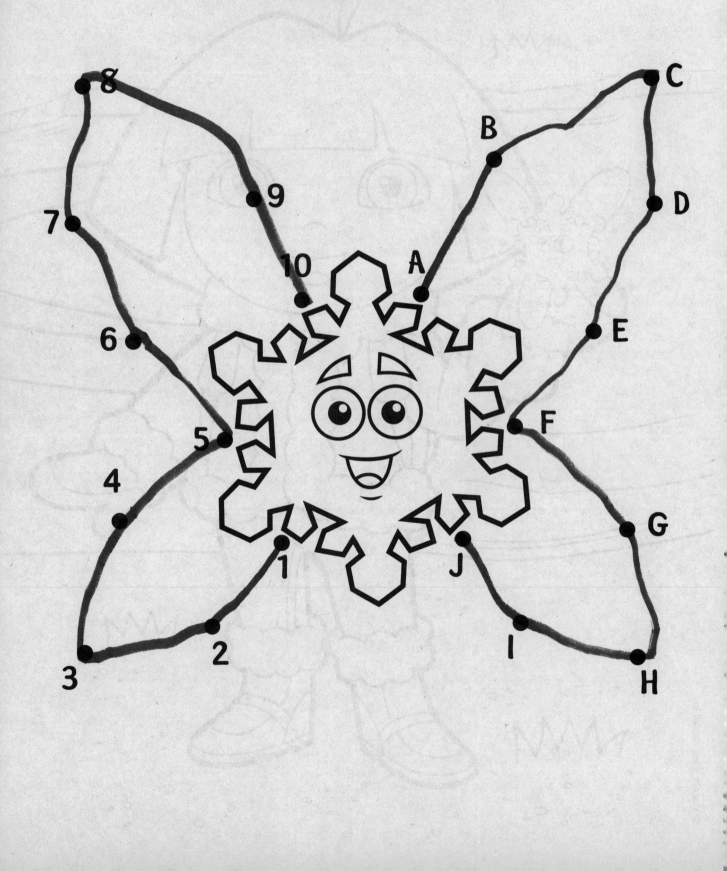

Thanks for helping the Snow Fairy fly.
He pulled the switch and lowered the
drawbridge. Now let's rescue the Princess!

We're Dora and Boots. We're here to rescue you
so you can smile into the crystal and save
the Snowy Forest!

The Princess says the Witch cast a spell on her.
She can't smile!

Sabrina thinks that since we look so much alike, maybe we should switch clothes. The Witch will think I'm Sabrina and maybe she'll show me the crystal!

But I'm not a princess.
What if the crystal doesn't work for me?

The Princess says the crystal works for her because she is brave and kind and helps her friends.

Oh, no! I hear the Witch coming, and there's no time to change clothes. But the Snow Fairy can help!

Quick! Hide from the Witch!

It's working! The Witch thinks I'm the Princess.
She says the Snowy Forest is almost gone
and will never come back.

She shows me the crystal, and I show her
that I can smile!

Help me break the spell by drawing
yourself with a really big smile!

We did it! The spell is broken!

And look, it's snowing!

The Witch's wand has snapped in half!
She'll never bother us again.

Without the Witch's power, the tower is disappearing. We've got to get out!

Yay! The Princess has been rescued!

The Snowy Forest is back!

The Snow Fairy is giving me a colorful new dress!

The Snow Fairy gave Boots new clothes, too!
Now he looks like a Snow Prince!
Use the key to color the fancy suit.

1 = Purple
2 = Blue
3 = Red
4 = Yellow
5 = Pink

The Snow Princess says the Snowy Forest could not have been saved without the help of her friends. She has medals for us!

¡Las medallas!

The Princess wants me to take care of the crystal.
I'll always protect it!

© Viacom International Inc.

Our new friend Pegasus is flying us home!

We saved the Princess and the Snowy Forest.
We couldn't have done it without you!
Thanks for helping. *¡Gracias!*

CRYSTAL KINGDOM

¡Hola! I'm Dora, and this is Boots!

We're going to read a story called "The Crystal Kingdom."

Once upon a time, there was a beautiful land filled with magic crystals. The crystals made everything colorful.

Everyone in the kingdom shared the crystals—except the Greedy King. He took the crystals and hid them in other stories!

**Without the crystals, the kingdom lost all its color.
A girl named Allie knew she had to find them.**

"Dora, your crystal is flashing!
It's shining a rainbow into the story."

Allie magically flew out of my book!

We have to help Allie find out where the Greedy King hid the crystals. Map can help us! Say "Map!"

"I'm Map. You have to go into Dora's stories and find the crystals hidden in Dragon Land, the Butterfly Cave, the Magic Cloud Castle, and the Crystal Kingdom."

First we have to go to Dragon Land.
Circle the story you think has a dragon in it.

Good work! We made it to Dragon Land.
Use the key to color the dragon.

1 = GREEN
2 = YELLOW
3 = RED

The Snow Princess, who gave me my necklace,
has a message: *To find the crystal,
we must save the fighting knight.*

**Look! The knight is fighting the dragon.
We have to stop him!**

Dragons only fight when they're scared.
If we can take away the knight's sword,
the dragon won't be scared!

"*¡Hola!* What can Dora use to pull the sword away from the knight? Will you circle it?"

Great work! Now help me lasso the sword.
Say "Lasso!"

Look! The dragon and the knight stopped fighting.
The dragon's really very kind.

The dragon knows where the Yellow Crystal is!
Help us find the way.

FINISH

START

We found the Yellow Crystal!
But here comes the Greedy King!
He wants it back.

Connect the dots so Kate the Knight can protect us from the Greedy King's magic!

Kate is giving us her shield to help us on our journey.
Let's go find the Green Crystal in the Butterfly Cave.

To jump into the second story,
say *"La segunda historia."*

There's the Butterfly Cave.
The Green Crystal is inside!

That giant caterpillar is stuck between those rocks.
How can we help her?

The Snow Princess has another message for us:
The caterpillar you can save by shining
sunlight into the cave.

We can bounce sunlight off
the shiny shield into the cave.

The sunlight warmed the caterpillar
and she became a butterfly!

The butterfly says the crystal is under cocoon number 12. Will you circle the correct cocoon?

1 2 3 4 5

6 7 8 9 10

11 12 13 14 15

The butterfly gave us magic wings to help us on our adventure. *¡Gracias, mariposa!*

The Blue Crystal is in the Magic Cloud Castle.

Enrique is a magician who lost his rabbits.
If you see 3 rabbits, will you circle them?

We're in the Magic Cloud Castle, looking for Enrique's hat. If you see it, will you circle it?

Yay! We found the Blue Crystal!

Enrique gave me a magic wand to help us find the last crystal in the fourth story. *¡La cuarta historia!*

"Dora, this is my home, the Crystal Kingdom.
It has lost so much color. We have to hurry!"

Look—on top of that volcano! It's the Greedy King, and the Red Crystal is in his crown!

Our wings will let us fly toward the Greedy King.
Flap your arms with us!

The Greedy King is using magic to throw volcano rocks at us! The shield will protect us!

Let's make our own magic spell.
Sing "Share, share, share."

It's working! The Greedy King's wand broke,
and the Red Crystal is floating toward us!

Use your crayons to help bring color back to the Crystal Kingdom.

We saved the Crystal Kingdom!

"Everyone is happy but me.
Maybe if I gave something away, I'd be happy, too."

The Greedy King wants to give Allie his crown.
Will you draw a crown on her head
to make her Queen?

The town threw us a party
to celebrate the return of the crystals.

We couldn't have saved
the Crystal Kingdom without you! ¡Gracias!

PRINCESS PUZZLES

Will you trace the lines and finish
Dora's royal costume?

Will you draw a castle for Princess Dora?

Will you find the path that goes all the way to the castle?

Will you connect the dots to make a crown for Dora?

Will you circle the two crowns that match?

Use the key to color Dora's magical carriage.

1 = PURPLE
2 = BLUE
3 = BROWN
4 = YELLOW
5 = PINK

Use the key to color Dora's beautiful princess gown.

1 = YELLOW
2 = BROWN
3 = PINK
4 = BLUE

Will you trace the dotted lines so Dora can become a Mermaid Princess?

Help Dora find her way to the dolphin.

FINISH

START

Will you circle the two gowns that match?

A

B

C

D

E

ANSWER: A and C.

Follow the path marked PRINCE to help Dora find the Prince.

Will you trace the lines to give Dora fairy princess wings?

Will you draw yourself as a princess?